ONE SNOWY
Night

Illustrated by
Alison Edgson

Stripes

CONTENTS

IN THE SNOWY MOUNTAINS

Linda Chapman

Amy gazed out of the plane window at the clear blue sky. She could still hear her best friend Olivia's astonished voice. "You're going to Mongolia in the Christmas holidays?"

Amy had nodded. Her mum was a wildlife journalist and had been asked to visit Mongolia to write an article about snow leopards. Amy was going with her and was really excited. Snow leopards were incredibly rare and the thought of seeing one in the wild was amazing!

"You'll have to tell me all about it when

you get back," Olivia had said enviously. She loved animals almost as much as Amy did.

"I will," Amy had promised.

When they arrived in Mongolia, Amy and her mum met up with Alex, a vet, and Sarnai and Ganzorig, the two scientists who were researching the snow leopards.

The team had hidden cameras across the mountains to film the leopards. Local herders were checking on the cameras, sending the data back to the team. The team's mission that week was to visit one of the locations for a few days, look at the cameras and try to tag any adult snow leopards they could find in order to keep track of them.

In the morning, they all piled into a jeep and set off to the herders' camp. After several hours they arrived in the foothills of a towering, snow-topped mountain. Amy caught her breath. There were long-horned sheep and shaggy ponies everywhere, being watched over by dark-haired people wearing long blue, brown and orange robes and sturdy sheepskin boots. The sound of baaing and bleating echoed across the valley as Amy got out of the jeep. The clear, cold air stung her cheeks and she was very glad of her thick winter coat, hat and gloves.

The herders lived in large, round cream-coloured tents called gers. Outside the gers more people were bustling about – some milking cattle, others carrying hay to the wooden pens or buckets of water. The children were helping too, sweeping up and grooming the shaggy ponies.

One of the men hurried over with a warm smile and greeted them in Mongolian.

"This is Batsuri," Alex, the vet, told Amy and her mum as the two scientists spoke to him. "He looks after the cameras for us in this area. You two will be staying with him and his wife, Dushmaa, while we will stay in another ger. Batsuri and Dushmaa speak some English."

Batsuri noticed Amy. "Hello, little one," he said. "You like?" He swept his arm around.

"Oh yes!" Amy breathed. "It's so beautiful! Thank you for having us to stay."

Batsuri smiled. "You are very welcome. Come." He pointed to a ger where a young woman was standing at the entrance.

"Please come in!" she called.

Everyone went inside. The walls of the ger were lined with colourful woollen rugs and there were more rugs spread on the floor. There were two wooden beds, covered with red and yellow throws, and in the centre was a stove – the chimney going out through the roof.

Hearing a bleating noise, Amy looked round in surprise. There was a pen in the ger with a black-and-white goat and a sheep in it. "You've got animals in here!" she said.

Dushmaa smiled. "Yes, we keep any sick

or weak animals with us so we can feed them and help them get better. Our animals are our friends. Now, please –" she smiled round at them all – "sit down and I'll get some tea."

Soon the team were drinking hot, milky tea. It was a bit of a squash in the ger but it was cosy and warm. Amy didn't understand much of the conversation as the team asked Batsuri questions about the snow leopards in Mongolian.

Dushmaa tapped Amy on the arm. "I am going to feed the animals. Would you like to help?"

Amy nodded eagerly. She helped Dushmaa put hay in pens and fill water troughs, then they groomed the ponies.

One of them – a fat brown pony called

Nartai – seemed restless. As Amy groomed her, Nartai stamped her hooves.

"Is she all right, Dushmaa?" Amy asked.

Dushmaa nodded at the mare's very round tummy. "She is going to have a foal soon. Maybe very soon."

In the afternoon, the team and Batsuri set off into the snowy mountains with a pony to carry their bags and equipment. Dushmaa gave Amy some strips of dried meat in case she got hungry.

After an hour's walking they reached a rocky area where Batsuri said he hoped they might see a snow leopard. A camera was hidden in a thorny bush. Over the previous seven months it had taken pictures of a snow leopard and her cub, but Batsuri was worried because there had been no pictures of them in the last few weeks. As the scientists examined the camera, Amy wandered a little further along the path.

"Don't go too far!" her mum called.

"I won't!" Amy called back.

She sat down on a rock near some trees and pulled out the dried meat. It was chewy but tasty. Suddenly a movement in the trees caught her attention. Two pale blue eyes were staring at her from the shadows. Amy froze. It was a young grey snow leopard about as big as a medium-sized dog but with a very long tail. Its eyes flicked hungrily to the meat in her hand. Amy wasn't scared. Her mum had told her snow leopards never attacked people. Moving slowly, she threw the meat on to the ground.

For a moment the skinny young leopard hesitated but then hunger got the better of it. Bounding out of the trees, it grabbed the meat then disappeared into the trees again, vanishing like a ghost. Amy leaped to her feet. She'd seen a snow leopard! Actually seen a real one in the wild! She ran to tell her mum.

When the scientists heard Amy's news

they were concerned. Snow leopards almost never approached humans. Something must be wrong. And where was the cub's mother? It was very young to be out alone. Amy's worries grew as she listened to them discussing the cub.

Alex gave Amy some more meat. "Let's see if it will come out again. It may be less scared of you because you are a child. The rest of us will stay back. If it does come, Batsuri will follow and try to find the den."

Amy placed the meat down by the trees and waited. *Please come*, she willed the cub.

There was a movement in the trees and the cub crept out. Delight rushed through Amy but she sat very still. The cub gobbled up the meat and then bounded away again.

But this time Batsuri was following.

"Now what?" Amy said, re-joining the others.

"Now we wait and see what Batsuri finds," her mum said grimly.

The minutes stretched by. Just when Amy felt she couldn't bear to wait any longer, Batsuri appeared. He spoke in rapid Mongolian, gesturing anxiously.

Alex translated. "Batsuri found the den. The mother is injured and looks in a bad way. The cub is too young to be able to hunt properly yet – they are starving."

Amy bit her lip. The poor snow leopards!

Batsuri leaped on to the pony.

"Where's he going?" Amy's mum asked.

"To get some fresh meat," said Sarnai. "He's left us a trail so we can go to the den and see if Alex can help the mother. Come on!"

The team followed the trail Batsuri had marked by tying strips of material to trees and bushes. They reached a cave in the mountainside. Alex crept forward with a tranquilizer gun. The darts in it would put the snow leopards to sleep for a little while so he could treat the injured mother.

Amy gripped her mum's hand. Could the team help the leopards? Had they got there in time?

"Finished!" Alex declared, cutting the last of the stitches that had been used to close up the nasty wound on the mother leopard's leg.

Both leopards were still asleep. The young cub was skinny but otherwise healthy. While Alex had worked, Amy and her mum had helped by holding lights and passing what was needed. Amy now crouched by the mother leopard. She longed to stroke her soft fur but she knew the leopards would not like to find the scent of humans on them when they woke up. They were wild, majestic animals, not pets. Amy gazed at them, taking in their pale fur with dark grey spots, their large fluffy paws and long tails. They were so beautiful.

Wearing gloves, Sarnai fixed a GPS collar to the mother's neck so they could track her movements. Meanwhile, Ganzorig had set up a camera on the cave wall so they could monitor the pair's progress after they left.

"Will the mother be OK?" Amy asked, looking at the sleeping leopards.

Alex nodded. "The wound will heal. She needs some food though."

Just then Batsuri arrived with a sackful of meat. "I will bring more tomorrow."

"Good, they'll be safe in this cave while the mother recovers." Alex smiled at Amy. "Thank you. By feeding the cub and getting it to come out you gave us a chance to work out what was going on. Without you, the world might have had two fewer snow leopards in it."

Amy felt a rush of happiness as she looked at the peaceful, sleeping cub. She hoped that one day, it too would have cubs of its own who would grow up to roam the mountain, wild and free.

By the time the team reached Batsuri's ger it was dusk. They were met with the delicious smell of lamb stew. Dushmaa wanted to know all the news.

"It was amazing," Amy began. "I saw a snow leopard cub and Batsuri tracked him and—"

She broke off with a gasp as she noticed that the animals in the pen had been joined by Nartai, the pony, and a tiny foal. She hurried over. "Nartai's had her baby!"

"Yes. I was right!" Dushmaa called.

"The foal was born this afternoon. I have brought them in here to keep them warm for the night."

Amy wished she could have a horse, sheep and goat in her home! *I really am going to have some good stories to tell Olivia,* she thought.

Her mum came over and hugged her. "Isn't it wonderful here?"

"Oh yes!" said Amy.

"Food time!" Dashmaa called.

Amy and her mum joined the others around the stove.

Meanwhile out on the mountain slopes, a snow leopard cub with a full tummy played while his mother watched over him. Above them, the bright Mongolian stars sparkled in the velvet-black sky.

WHAT'S
HAPPENED TO
WINTER?

Liss Norton

It was the day before the rabbits' skating party but there was no ice on the pond.

"What's happened to winter?" said Clover with a sigh. She gazed out of the window and scratched her soft brown ears anxiously. "There's not even a sniff of snow."

Every year the rabbits held an ice skating party to celebrate midwinter but this year the summer had stretched on and on. The trees were still full of green leaves and butterflies still danced among the flowers.

Clover's friend Dandelion, a grey rabbit with a very twitchy nose, shook his head.

"I checked the pond on my way here," he said, "and there's no ice at all, just water. The party will have to be cancelled."

"No way!" said Clover in a determined voice. "Everyone's been looking forward to it for so long." Last year had been her first skating party but she could still remember the thrill of whizzing round the pond by twinkling lantern light, and tucking into hot carrot pasties.

Clover's grandad was reading the Rabbit News. "Do you know why winter hasn't come, Grandad?" Clover asked.

"It's Jack Frost's job to bring snow and ice," he replied. "But he seems to have forgotten us this year."

"Someone needs to remind him then," said Clover. She took Dandelion's paw and led him outside. "Let's go and find Jack Frost and ask him to bring winter here, to Rabbit Valley."

Dandelion's eyes shone with excitement. "Do you think we can? Oh, Clover, that would be such a big adventure!"

"Of course we can," said Clover. "If we go far enough north, we'll find Jack Frost. I'm sure of it!"

They packed carrot sandwiches and thick jumpers into a backpack. "Here we go then," Clover said excitedly as they set off.

They walked a long way, through shady woods, across fields of tickly grass and up and down steep hills, but there was no sign of winter anywhere.

At lunchtime, just as they finished their sandwiches in Hedgehog Wood, a hedgehog family came to see them. They looked very tired. "Do you know what's happened to winter?" they asked, yawning. "We're ready to hibernate but it's not cold enough."

"We think Jack Frost's forgotten to come this year," Clover said. "When we find him, we'll ask him to bring winter here, as well as to Rabbit Valley."

She and Dandelion hurried on, but all too soon the sun began to sink. "It's nearly night," Dandelion sighed. "We should give up and go home."

"Let's go just a bit further," said Clover. "Maybe Jack's over the next hill." She couldn't bear to think of heading home without finding him.

They raced up the hill, still searching for any sign of winter, but they'd both begun to think that it was hopeless. "We'll turn back if we can't see anything from the top," Clover said sadly.

They reached the top of the hill and stood gazing around while they got their breath back. The setting sun cast long rosy shadows across the land.

"Look at that castle," Dandelion said, pointing to an enormous building that glinted pale pink in the sun's rays. It had tall spiral towers topped with sharp spikes and the windows glittered with frost. A fir tree stood beside the front door. It was covered in snow and more snow lay on the ground.

Clover's heart began to pound. "That castle looks as though it's made of ice!" she cried. "It must be Jack Frost's castle. Come on, Dandelion!"

They raced down the hill. With every step the air grew colder and their breath puffed out of their mouths in icy clouds. Reaching the castle's front door, they could see that the whole building really was made of shimmering ice. Clover jangled the bell that hung beside the door.

"Who's that?" croaked a weak voice from inside.

"Clover and Dandelion from Rabbit Valley," Clover replied. "We're looking for Jack Frost."

"Come in!" the voice called. "I'm upstairs in bed with a terrible cold."

Clover and Dandelion exchanged excited looks. "We've found him!" breathed Clover. She opened the door and they stepped into a wide entrance hall with a flight of glittering ice stairs leading up.

"I'm glad we brought our jumpers," Dandelion said, shivering. He pulled his on and Clover did the same.

"I've never been anywhere as c-c-cold as this before," she said through chattering teeth.

They scampered upstairs and found Jack Frost. He was lying in bed with the blankets pulled up to his chin. He had long, sharp fingers, pointed ears and hair that stood up in icy spikes. His skin was pale blue and ice crystals clung to it. He was shivering violently.

Clover was shocked to see how ill he looked. "Can we do something for you?" she asked.

"I'd love a mug of cocoa and could you light the fire, please," he replied. "I don't usually feel the cold but I just can't get warm today."

The wood was already laid in the fireplace. Clover lit it and watched, pleased, as flames sprang up, warming the room.

Dandelion ran down to the kitchen and made cocoa for them all.

They sat by Jack's bed and sipped their steaming drinks. "I feel a bit better already, thanks to you," Jack said, setting down his empty mug. "Now tell me why you've come."

"We wanted to ask why you hadn't brought winter to Rabbit Valley," Clover explained. "Tomorrow's the day of our midwinter skating party but there's no ice on the pond. We can see you're too ill to go out, though."

"I am," Jack said. "I'm very sorry to spoil your party. My winter crystals are ready to scatter but I don't feel well enough to get out of bed."

Clover's heart skipped a beat. "I've got

an idea," she said. "Can we scatter the crystals for you?"

Jack's blue eyes brightened. "Of course you can! That's a wonderful idea. My crystals are in a basket on my sledge, which you can find parked round the back of the castle. Sprinkle them as you go along and winter will spring up all around you."

"Let's do it now!" cried Clover. "Come on, Dandelion. There's not a moment to lose."

They said goodbye, promising to come again with the sledge to check that Jack was all right, then dashed downstairs and round to the back of the castle. Jack's sledge was beautifully carved from a single block of greeny-blue ice and held a basket filled to the brim with glittering crystals. Clover threw a pawful of them into the air and snowflakes began to whirl around them like tiny ballerinas in frilly white dresses. The two friends watched, entranced, as they settled thickly on the ground.

"Let's go," Clover said. She could hardly wait to get back to Rabbit Valley with the precious winter crystals, but they had to spread winter everywhere else as they went along too.

Dandelion pulled the sledge while Clover tossed the ice crystals this way and that. They reached Hedgehog Wood and all the hedgehogs came running to meet them. "You've brought winter," they cheered as Clover scattered more crystals and snow began to fall. "Thanks! Now we can start our long winter sleep."

"You're welcome," Dandelion said. "Sweet dreams!"

The two friends ran on and on, spreading winter far and wide. It was dark now but the shining moon set the snow gleaming so brightly that it was easy to see the way.

At last they finally reached Rabbit Valley. "Oh no!" gasped Clover. "Jack's basket is almost empty!"

Dandelion peered anxiously into the basket. The few crystals that were left looked very small and they weren't as sparkly as the ones they'd scattered before. "Throw them close to the pond," he said. "Even if there aren't enough to make it snow, they might freeze the water so we can still skate."

Clover scooped up the last few crystals and placed them carefully around the pond. She held her breath as she waited to see what would happen, but nothing changed. No snowflakes fell, no ice appeared on the pond.

"I can't believe we went all that way and spread winter everywhere, but didn't keep enough for Rabbit Valley," she said sadly. "The skating party really will be cancelled."

Miserably, she and Dandelion trudged back to their burrows and went to bed.

Clover woke late the next day. She remembered at once about running out of crystals. *Why didn't I save enough for Rabbit Valley?* she thought unhappily.

Suddenly she heard a cheerful shout outside. "Got you!"

Clover sprang out of bed and flung open her curtains. The ground was blanketed with deep snow and her friends were building snow rabbits and throwing snowballs.

Clover dashed outside. "Is the pond frozen?" she called.

"Frozen solid," her friends chorused. "Winter's come at last!"

A shiver of excitement ran through Clover, from her ears to the soles of her feet. The crystals had worked after all!

That night Clover, Mum and Grandad put on their warmest clothes and headed for the pond. The way was lit with twinkling lanterns that made the snow sparkle, and the path was crowded with their friends and relations all hurrying to the party.

Dandelion came running up, holding tight to his ice skates. "I can't wait for the party to start!" he cried.

"Me neither," agreed Clover. The snow was deep and the air was cold – it hardly seemed possible that yesterday had been as warm as summer.

They reached the frozen pond and gazed in delight at the flickering lanterns and the tables piled high with cakes, pies, cookies and jugs of steaming blackberry juice. A band was playing merry music, and the air was full of the smell of roasting chestnuts and toasting marshmallows.

"Thank goodness we found Jack Frost!"
Clover said.

"Let's visit him again tomorrow to take
back the sledge and to make sure he's OK,"
suggested Dandelion.

"Good idea," agreed Clover as she tied
the laces of her skates. "But let's not wish
for tomorrow to come too soon. I'm going
to enjoy every single second of this party.
It'll be a night to remember!"

A CHRISTMAS STAR

Holly Webb

Lucy peered round the edge of the living-room door. "Can I come in yet?" she asked hopefully. The coffee table was covered with rolls of glittery wrapping paper and there were odds and ends of it all over the floor.

Her mum laughed. "Don't worry, Lucy, all the presents are wrapped up and under the tree now."

"Thank goodness..." said Lucy's dad, stretching his hands into star shapes and waving them. "I've got scissor-cramp. Perhaps we should take some of these presents back, I think there are too many."

"Da-aad! But really? Are there lots?" Lucy asked hopefully.

"Look." He beckoned her in and pointed to the Christmas tree. Lucy caught her breath. It was beautiful anyway, with golden lights twinkling all over it and fat ropes of tinsel, but now it was surrounded with piles and piles of presents.

"Wow…" Lucy whispered. There really were a lot. And some of them were huge. Suddenly a little furry face appeared, determinedly heaving itself up over the top of the biggest box. It let out a tiny breathless mew.

"Oh, that's where you are!" Mum sighed. "Lucy, your kitten thinks that tree is her own personal playground. She nearly got to the top last time."

"Sorry…" Lucy giggled. "I thought she was asleep in her basket in the kitchen. Hey, Star! Come on, come here, puss." She scooped the little grey-and-white tabby up in her arms, and Star shot out a paw to dab at a dangling end of tinsel. She adored the Christmas tree. As far as she could see, it was a climbing frame and a whole lot of cat toys all built into one sparkly, exciting bundle. She looked back regretfully as

Lucy carried her away.

"Mum, can I wrap my presents now?" Lucy asked. She had one for Mum and Dad that she'd made at school – a calendar for next year that she had worked really hard on. It had a drawing of Star on it and Mr Dixon, her teacher, had told her it was brilliant. She was really looking forward to giving it to Mum and Dad tomorrow. She had a bag of her grandad's favourite toffee to wrap up too.

"Sure." Her mum smiled. "Does that mean we have to leave the room?"

Lucy nodded, giggling. "It's a secret. You go in the kitchen and I'll get the presents from upstairs."

Mum nodded. "If you wrap your presents now, sweetheart, we can clear all the wrapping paper away. Then maybe we can watch a film or play a game?"

Lucy nodded. She put Star down on the arm of the sofa and the kitten promptly jumped off to investigate the ribbon dangling out of the wrapping-paper box.

Wrapping was hard, Lucy realized, ten minutes later. It was even harder when you had a kitten who was determined to help. She lifted Star off the roll of wrapping paper for the third time and waved the ribbon from the wrapping box at her. "Not again, Star! Look! Look, Star! Sparkly!"

The kitten bounced off the table and flung herself at the coiling end of ribbon, rolling over on to her back and catching it with her claws. Then she chewed it thoroughly. It was quite hard work and by the time she'd got it nibbled to bits, she was starting to feel sleepy.

Now that Star was busy with the ribbon, Lucy quickly cut along the paper and started to fold it round her calendar. Grandad's toffee was tricky – it was bulgy in all the wrong places.

Lucy looked at her presents critically. They weren't too bad. The paper was nice anyway – white with gold snowflakes on. She put them under the tree with the others. Then she put the roll of paper and the tape back in the cardboard box and tucked the ribbon back in too. Hopefully no one would notice that it was a bit chewed...

"Oh, are you done? Great. I'll put this back under the stairs." Dad picked up the wrapping-paper box and Lucy opened the cupboard door for him. The cupboard was quite full and the box only just fitted back in.

Exciting, lovely things just seemed to keep happening that evening. Dad had made a beautiful Christmas cake, topped with mountains of snowy icing, and Father Christmas and a troop of penguins on skis. They left a mince pie and a flask of coffee for Father Christmas by the fireplace, and some carrots for the reindeer. Lucy wanted to put them on the garage roof because she reckoned it would be a really good sleigh parking place, but Mum decided the garden would have more room for all the reindeer.

At bedtime, Mum brought out some new pyjamas with glow in the dark stars on. Everything was perfect. Until Lucy snuggled up with Mum to read together and said, "Where's Star?"

Her mum looked around, surprised. "Oh, you're right, she's not here. Perhaps she's finishing off her dinner. I'm sure she'll be up soon."

"But – but I haven't fed Star her dinner!" Lucy cried, her eyes widening. "I forgot, because of the cake and playing Pictionary and all the Christmassy things… And she always comes and asks for her tea but she didn't. She hasn't mewed at me – I haven't even seen her!"

"I did give her a bit of bacon this afternoon, when I was getting the food ready for tomorrow," Lucy's mum murmured. "But you're right, it is strange. Dave, have you seen Star anywhere?" she asked Lucy's dad, who'd put his head round the door to say goodnight.

He looked surprised. "No... Not for ages actually."

"I'll go and look for her," Lucy said. "She must be starving."

Lucy had half expected Star to come running as soon as she came downstairs, making little starving kitten wailing noises. But she didn't. She wasn't in the kitchen or the living room. Dad even went back upstairs and checked to make sure he hadn't shut her in his and Mum's room. She wasn't anywhere.

Star's cat flap was on a timer so she

couldn't go out at night but she had been known to sneak out if someone opened the door. "I took those bits of wrapping paper out to the recycling bin," Dad murmured. "I didn't see her follow me, though. I'm sure I would have noticed. Let's go and call her just in case."

Lucy pulled on her wellies and coat over her pyjamas, and they stood in the front garden, calling Star's name and shaking a packet of cat treats. Lucy was waiting to see a little grey shadow come trotting down the path but the garden was silent and still. No one was around and it was so cold.

"This is no good," Dad said. "I don't think she's out here – she usually comes running if she hears the treats packet rustling, doesn't she?"

"Can we just try for a bit longer?" Lucy pleaded. "She might be coming. She could be in next-door's garden," she added hopefully, peering over at the fences on both sides.

They shook the treats again and Lucy made puss, puss, puss noises, but Star was nowhere to be seen. At last she had to let Dad persuade her back in.

They searched the house again. Lucy even opened up her wardrobe and the boxes where all her toys were stored, just in case. No cross little kitten popped out.

"Lucy, it's getting late," Mum said gently. "I think you'd better go to bed. I'm sure Star will pop in through the cat flap any minute now."

Lucy stared at her. "But I can't go to

sleep! What if something's happened to her?" She sniffed back tears. "I haven't seen her since I was wrapping your present – that's ages. She could have run out into the street and – and…" She didn't even want to think about it.

"Hang on." Dad turned round from the back door, where he'd been peering out into the garden. "She was there when you were wrapping presents?"

"Yes." Lucy's voice wobbled. "She kept sitting on the wrapping paper. And then she ate the ribbon. I was grumpy with her! Maybe she decided to go out because I wouldn't let her play."

Dad smiled and shut the back door. "I've just thought of somewhere we haven't looked."

Lucy shook her head. "We've searched everywhere, Dad, honestly."

"Nope." Dad led the way back into the hall and crouched down by the cupboard under the stairs. Very gently he reached in and pulled out the box of wrapping paper, putting it down at Lucy's feet. "I remember thinking this was really heavy when I put it away," he told Lucy, grinning.

Lucy crouched down and peered into the box, lifting up the packet of shiny ribbon rosettes on the top. Curled up on a wodge of star-printed wrapping paper was Star, fast asleep, with that same bit of chewed up ribbon wrapped around her paws.

"Oh Star!" Lucy whispered. "I was so worried. We didn't know where you were! I must have put those rosettes on top of her!"

"I expect she got a bit bored and found a cosy place to sleep," Mum said, laughing. "I'll go and get her dinner, she'll be starving now."

Lucy reached into the box and picked up her kitten, all warm and floppy with sleep, and Star opened one eye lazily. She gave a huge yawn and shook her ears – and then she heard the cat biscuits hitting her bowl. She wriggled out of Lucy's arms, racing for the kitchen.

"You'd better get to bed, Lucy," Dad said, giving her a hug. "Don't worry. I'll bring her up to you in a bit."

Lucy trailed up the stairs, suddenly so tired. *It's Christmas Eve!* she thought, with a last little jump of excitement as she climbed into bed. *Presents* – her stocking was there ready. She snuggled the duvet up round her shoulders.

A little later, she shifted and smiled as a small furry body curled in next to her, and a rough pink tongue licked her cheek.

"We couldn't have Christmas without you," she whispered to her kitten, and Star purred back.

MIMOO AND MUM-MUM

Candy Gourlay

Mimoo was a baby panda. Mum-Mum was her mother and they lived in a great forest of yellow bamboo on a tall, pointed mountain in China.

Mimoo was a tiny little thing, with wee ears that had barely turned black and a round, furry body. Mum-Mum, on the other hand, was a Giant Panda. Mum-Mum looked exactly the way one might imagine a Giant Panda would look: giant ... and a panda.

Mimoo was born in the spring time, when the forest floor was covered with yellow and purple flowers and, by the time the hot summer began, she was ready to learn how to climb the tall yellow canes of the bamboo forest.

All summer, Mum-Mum took Mimoo up to the tops of the waving bamboo, teaching her how to pull herself up the canes, which were slender but strong. She showed Mimoo how to pick the stalks from the canes and where the tastiest bits could be found. Mimoo climbed and ate and grew stronger and bigger. Even so, next to her giant mother, she was still a tiny panda.

The weather turned again and the mountain breeze suddenly seemed to grow teeth that nibbled on Mimoo's little nose.

"Are you cold, my little Mimoo?" Mum-Mum asked.

Now, despite her giant size, Mum-Mum had the wispiest voice and Mimoo often did not catch what she was saying the first time.

"Sorry?" Mimoo said.

"I said," Mum-Mum whispered. "Are you chilly?"

Mimoo wasn't sure what chilly was. But she nodded, thinking that was the answer Mum-Mum wanted. Instead of looking pleased, Mum-Mum looked up worriedly at the sky.

"I thought so," she said softly. "I think it's time."

Time? Mimoo wondered. *Time for what?*

At that moment, Mimoo spotted a white feather wafting down from the sky.

It must have been dropped by a bird.

Down it drifted. Down, down, down …
until it landed on Mimoo's nose.

It was icy when Mimoo touched
it. When she removed her paw,
the feather had vanished.
All that was left was a
dab of wetness on the tip
of her nose.

Another feather
drifted down and Mimoo
clapped both paws over
it. When she opened them,
this feather had vanished as
well! Where her paws had touched it, she
felt a cold tingle. Like a little kiss.

There was white cloud hovering over
the mountain peak. The feathers were
coming from it, falling faster and faster,

65

and swirling together in fierce clumps.

"What is it, Mum-Mum?" Mimoo breathed.

Mum-Mum smiled. "Snow," she whispered. "It is snow. When snow comes, it is time to go down the mountain."

"Go down?" Mimoo said. She had never gone down the mountain before. "Why?"

"It will be warmer there. And there will be no snow."

"But I like the snow!"

"Snow is pretty," Mum-Mum whispered. "But we are pandas and pandas move to where it's warmer when the weather gets cold."

Mum-Mum plucked Mimoo from her perch and popped her on her back. The canes rustled and whispered as she began to make her way down the mountain.

Mimoo stared, open mouthed, as they moved into a strange new world. The bamboo was replaced by trees she had never seen before. Every branch wore heavy sleeves of snow. And the forest floor had completely disappeared under a thick white blanket. Every boulder wore a funny white cap. Everywhere, pillows of snow lay, fat and inviting.

Mimoo couldn't resist. She jumped from Mum-Mum's back into a snowdrift, sending clumps of snow flying.

"Look, Mum-Mum!" she squealed. "This is fun!"

"Mimoo!" Mum-Mum raised her whispery voice but it wasn't very loud.

"We cannot stay here!"

"Just one more time, Mum-Mum!" she cried, running toward another snow mound.

"Mimoo!" Mum-Mum shouted. "We must—"

But the little panda had jumped again.

The snow wrapped around Mimoo's furry little body like a big hug. The snow shuddered and then the great snow hug rolled over, taking Mimoo with it.

"Wheeeee!" Mimoo squealed as she began to tumble down the mountain in the middle of the snowy lump. She glimpsed Mum-Mum's face, eyes wide with alarm and mouth open as she ran after her.

"Mimoo!" She heard Mum-Mum cry.

Mimoo kicked but she couldn't stop the snow thing rolling. At first she could see bright flashes of sky and tree as she rolled. But then she began gathering snow and soon she found herself tightly packed into a giant snowball. All she could see was white, white, white.

And then suddenly the snowball bounced once, twice, then came to a stop.

Mimoo wriggled and jiggled until she

managed to push her head out of the ball.
Where was she?

The ball had rolled into a cave. There
was a faint glow from the cave's mouth and
blinking at her were two sleepy eyes.

In the dim light, a massive body uncurled,
stretching great big arms above its head.

"Hello," a gruff voice said. "Who are
you?"

The face that looked down at her was
a great shaggy thing with drooping eyes.
It yawned, baring two neat rows of sharp
teeth.

"I'm Mimoo!" Mimoo cried.

"Why, hello, Mimoo." The shaggy brown
head moved closer. "My name is Pao. You
have bear ears and bear fur. Just like me."

Mimoo stared. Pao was not as big as

Mum-Mum. She was not as round as Mum-Mum. She did not even smell like Mum-Mum. She was brown all over.

"I'm a panda!" Mimoo said.

"What are you doing in my cave? Were you looking for somewhere to sleep?"

"I was in a snowball," Mimoo explained. "And it rolled here. Is this the bottom of the mountain?"

"No," Pao said. "It's only halfway down."

"Good!" Mimoo cried. "Mum-Mum will be here soon."

She turned and scrambled towards the mouth of the cave.

The bear lumbered slowly after her. "Where are you going?"

"I have to wait for Mum-Mum outside so that she can see me," Mimoo said.

Pao yawned and shook her head. "You're a very small bear. You shouldn't be out there on your own. Anyway, it's snowing. When it snows, bears go to sleep."

"I'm a panda!" Mimoo said crossly. "Anyway, Mum-Mum should be here soon. She was chasing after me."

The bear followed Mimoo out.

"Mum-Mum!" she called.

"Shh!" the bear said. "Don't make so much noise. The yellow-throated martens will hear you!"

"What are yellow-throated martens?"

"You don't want to run into one. Yellow throats. Black heads." The bear yawned again. "Nasty things with sharp, bitey teeth!"

The bear settled down next to Mimoo. "Let me wait here with you until your

Mum-Mum comes. I'll help you look out for those martens. It's the least a bear can do for another bear."

"Thank you," Mimoo said as the bear settled her great bulk into the snow next to her. "But I'm a panda."

The bear was not listening. Pao had tucked her chin into her chest. Her eyes were closed.

"Pao?" Mimoo said.

The bear began to snore. "*Zzzzzzzz.*"

Mimoo sighed and leaned her head against Pao's warm shoulder. If Pao was asleep, how was she going to help if those martens turned up?

"Ahem." Someone behind a boulder cleared his throat.

Three slim figures stepped out from

behind the boulder.

They had black heads and yellow throats.

"Pao!" Mimoo whispered. "Wake up!"

But the bear continued to snore.

The yellow throats of the martens shone bright against the white of the snow. Their long black tails quivered and their button eyes gleamed.

"I can see a sleeping bear!" said one.

"And next to the bear, what can you see?" said the second.

"I can see..." the third one began.

"A panda!" the three of them exclaimed together.

The first one licked his lips. "And what do we think of baby pandas, my friends?"

The second marten grinned. "We think baby pandas are yummy!"

"Yes we do!" the third marten said.

Mimoo gave up trying to wake the bear. She got to her feet, puffing out her chest. "Go away!" she cried fiercely. "Or my bear friend will fight you!"

The three martens roared with laughter.

"It's snowing and that bear is fast asleep," one said.

Mimoo tried to ignore her pounding

heart. "Well, my mum is bigger than all of you put together. And she's going to be here soon!"

"Going to be here soon?" The martens began to advance on Mimoo, long tails swishing and pointy teeth showing. "Then we have no time to waste!"

Suddenly there was an ear-splitting *"ROAAAAAAAAAAAR!"*

The three martens leaped high in the air in fright. Clumps of snow jumped off the trees as if they were scared too.

"LEAVE MIMOO ALONE – NOW! – OR YOU ARE GOING TO BE SORRY!"

"It's the panda's mum!" the martens squeaked, scuttling into the bushes.

Mimoo gulped. Who could be shouting from behind the tree? It definitely wasn't

Mum-Mum!

But the creature who leaped out was giant and furred in black and white – Mum-Mum!

Mum-Mum snatched Mimoo into her arms, tucking her great furry chin over her head. She kissed each of Mimoo's ears and rocked her in her arms. The little panda clung tightly to her mum's fur.

"Oh Mimoo," Mum-Mum said in her whispery voice. "You rolled so far down the mountain it took me a long time to catch up! Were you scared?"

Mimoo stared at her mother. "Mum-Mum!" she said. "Your voice didn't sound like you at all! How did you do that?"

Mum-Mum laughed. "Why, that wasn't me, sweet Mimoo. That was my friend. Here he is."

And for the first time, Mimoo noticed a tiny brown creature with standing-up grey ears. "This is my friend Chu," Mum-Mum said. "He's a pika. He may be small but he's got a great big voice."

"HAPPY TO HELP!" the tiny creature said. "WE PIKAS MAY BE SMALL BUT WE CAN MAKE A BIG SOUND."

Pao suddenly stirred and opened one eye. "Keep it down, Chu, I'm trying to sleep!"

"WAKEY WAKEY!" Chu grabbed the bear's arm. "LET ME TAKE YOU BACK TO YOUR DEN, BEAR. IT WON'T DO TO SLEEP THE WINTER AWAY OUT HERE IN THE OPEN."

As Chu helped the bear get on to her feet, Mum-Mum thanked them both: Chu for being her voice, and the bear for watching over Mimoo (even if she had fallen asleep).

With Chu's help, the bear shuffled sleepily back into her cave. Mum-Mum tucked Mimoo on to her broad back and they continued their journey to the bottom of the mountain where there was another forest of scrumptious bamboo.

"Go to sleep, darling," Mum–Mum whispered. "We'll be there soon."

Mimoo gazed up at the white puffy cloud still sprinkling snow on the world below. What a day she'd had!

Bye bye, snow, she thought sleepily, wondering what tomorrow was going to bring.

A WINTER
SURPRISE

Swapna Haddow

It was dawn and all was still in the sleepy burrows of Cherry Tree Woods. Not a single mouse nor a single hedgehog stirred. Each and every creature was tucked up cosy in their den, dreaming dreams of winter fun and snowy adventures. All apart from a ground squirrel, Jumbie, who had been awake all night.

Jumbie was on a hunt. He searched through the tunnels of his burrow. He searched to the left. He searched to the right. He searched high. He searched low.

"Where did I put them?" Jumbie thought

out loud to himself, scratching his chin.

Across the room, tiny triangles of bunting were strung up from long feather reeds. The table was decorated with acorn hats and a glorious bouquet of winter's greenery. The scent of fresh pine filled the air. The delicious smell of roasting chestnuts and baking nutmeg started to drift from the stove. This was going to be the perfect surprise winter woodland party for his friends and Jumbie was so proud of preparing everything all by himself.

But now the invitations were nowhere to be found. What a shock Jumbie had had when he discovered this on the way to the post box earlier that evening. There couldn't be a party without invites. Jumbie had been looking for them ever since. He had to find them.

He continued to hunt through his home. He clattered around in his stores of berries. He dug through his hoards of nuts. He rummaged under his bed and inside his moss-filled duvet.

"Where, oh where did I put them?"

His rummaging and clattering had woken up his neighbour Horris, who was the sort of hedgehog who liked to investigate rummagings and clatterings.

Horris rolled out of bed and followed the noise straight to Jumbie's front door. He had to knock several times before he could be heard over all the hullabaloo.

"Horris!" Jumbie said, when he finally opened the door. "How can I help you?"

"I heard so much noise coming from

your burrow, I came over to see if everything was all right?"

Horris arched his neck, trying to look into Jumbie's home but the squirrel shielded the entrance of his house with his body. He'd spent days getting the surprise party ready and he wasn't about to let Horris in on the secret just yet.

"Everything is fine," Jumbie said, but his furrowed brow and hunched shoulders said otherwise and his good friend Horris knew something was wrong.

"Jumbie," Horris said, looking concerned. "What's the matter?"

"Oh, Horris," Jumbie said, his voice

small. "I've lost something important."

"What is it?" Horris asked. "Can I help you find it?"

Before he said anything further, Jumbie stopped. He didn't want any help. He'd put together the entire party himself. He could find the invitations all by himself.

"There is absolutely nothing to worry about," Jumbie said, forcing a smile. "I don't need any help."

"Are you sure?"

"It's all in hand, Horris, my friend," Jumbie said. "I'm very sorry for waking you."

"Oh, it's no bother, Jumbie. It's morning now and I have to pick up breakfast for the hoglets from Miss Buttermitten's soon."

Miss Buttermitten!

Jumbie remembered seeing the invitations when he had stopped by for a berry tea and a much needed rest, while running party errands the day before.

Of course! That must have been where he'd left them.

"I'm sorry, Horris, but I must rush to Miss Buttermitten's at once!"

"But—"

"Goodbye, Horris."

Horris headed home and Jumbie bounded off to Miss Buttermitten's.

The lights hanging from the tree branches outside Miss Buttermitten's café twinkled like stars. Jumbie brushed the snow from his coat and stepped into the warm, bright shop, which was filled with smells of cinnamon buns baking and stewed winter berries simmering on the cooker.

"Good morning, Jumbie," Miss Buttermitten said. The long-tailed mole's cheeks were pink from the warm kitchen. "How can I help?"

"I don't need any help thanks, Miss Buttermitten," Jumbie said, waving away his friend.

Miss Buttermitten watched as Jumbie looked under tables and pushed aside chairs. He searched behind the benches and plush cushions.

"Are you sure I can't help, Jumbie?" Miss Buttermitten asked again. "Is there something you're looking for?"

"There is absolutely nothing to worry about," Jumbie said. "I don't need any help at all."

Jumbie stopped and looked up from the "Lost Property" box, which was filled with forgotten toys and odd woolly mittens. His tail drooped. There was no sign of the lost invitations.

He pulled out an ice skate. He used his paw to rub off a spot of rust on the blade before dropping the skate back in the box. Of course! After he had been at Miss Buttermitten's the previous day, he had gone to see his friend Artie for an afternoon of ice skating on the pond. That was where he'd seen his invitations last.

Jumbie quickly brushed down his fur.

"If you tell me what you are looking for, I can help you find it," Miss Buttermitten offered.

"Don't worry," Jumbie said. He dashed for the door, leaving Miss Buttermitten shaking her head in confusion. "I've just remembered I must go and see Artie immediately."

Jumbie sprung across the snowy woodland, leaping from one icy tree stump to the next. The snow crunched under his paws as he hurdled over frost-covered toadstools and frozen twigs.

By the time he arrived at Artie's, there was a queue for the ice-rink pond. Jumbie drummed his foot on the floor as he waited behind baby mice and little squirrel kittens who sang songs about the winter and chattered excitedly.

He tapped and twitched, gritting his teeth. When his friends and neighbours greeted him in the queue, he hrumpf-ed and grunted, annoyed by their happy smiles and kind words.

"Finally!" Jumbie said, as he reached the front of the queue.

"Jumbie?" Artie exclaimed. The toad was surprised by his friend's curt greeting. "Are you here to skate again?"

"No!" Jumbie snapped. "I have to search the pond."

He took to the ice, sweeping across the frozen surface, dashing around in a panic.

"Watch out, Mr Jumbie!" Horris' two youngest hoglets shouted, as they slipped on the ice and careered into the squirrel.

Jumbie cartwheeled across the ice and
landed in a heap at the edge of the pond.
His friends raced towards him as he rubbed
the bump on his head.

"Jumbie?" Artie asked. "Are you OK?"

Jumbie shook his head.

"Let me help you," Horris said as he
bent down to help the squirrel up.

A tear slipped out and trailed down Jumbie's cheek as he pushed his friend away.

"I don't need any help!"

Artie and Horris took a step back, and Jumbie could see the hurt on their faces.

What had he done?

He had planned a party for his friends but now as they looked at him in dismay, he realized he was pushing away the very friends he wished to honour.

His chin trembled and tears streamed down his cheeks.

"I wanted to surprise you all!" Jumbie cried out. "I wanted to put on the best surprise winter woodland party tonight."

Before anyone could say anything, Jumbie let out a wail. "But I lost all the invitations!"

"Oh, Jumbie," Artie said, pulling his friend up into a hug.

"It's OK," one of the little mice put in. "We can help you find them."

"Yes," agreed Artie. "If we look together, we can find them."

"Or we could help you make new ones?" Horris suggested.

"What a great idea," Miss Buttermitten said, catching the end of the conversation as she arrived at the pond.

"But there's no time," Jumbie said, in a wobbly voice.

Horris crouched down next to his friend.

"I bet it will be a magnificent party anyway, even without the invitations," Horris said.

Jumbie looked around. The faces of his

friends were full of love and understanding, and he realized then that Horris was right. He didn't need his invitations. Everyone he dearly loved was standing around him. Everyone he wanted to invite to the party.

"I'm so sorry I've been in such a grump of a mood," he said, his voice barely louder than a whisper. "I've been ever so rude to you all."

"It's OK," Miss Buttermitten said. "You must have worked hard on your surprise party."

"I did," Jumbie said. "I wanted it to be perfect."

Jumbie reached out his paw to Horris. He looked at his neighbour's kind face and knew the perfect way to say sorry.

"Come with me," Jumbie said, with a

huge smile. "Follow me, everyone."

Jumbie led his friends back to his burrow where they found it covered in beautiful bunting. The table was decorated with acorn hats and the air was filled with the delicious smells of fresh pine, roasting chestnuts and baked nutmeg.

"Welcome to my surprise winter woodland party," said Jumbie. He beamed as his friends delighted in their special celebration and cheered their squirrel friend. There was dancing and singing. Jumbie taught his friends his favourite games of Catch The Acorn and Hide and Go Seek until late into the evening. It was the best surprise winter woodland party they had ever had.

A ROBIN'S WELCOME

Sita Brahmachari

"One snowy night…"

That is how everyone in my class must start to tell a story for homework.

"But all the stories will be the same!" my friend Femi complains.

"I don't think so, Femi. They'll be like snowflakes. Imagine — not a single one has the same formation and yet they all make snow!" Miss Willow looks to the window. "It's forecast over the weekend…"

Femi sighs and drama-drops her head on to the table.

"I'll tell you what, Year Four," Miss

Willow says. "If it snows there's no homework except to play outside!"

We walk home through the park together, eyes up. Sky is white ... heavy and waiting.

"I wish it would snow!" Femi says and pulls the ends of my red scarf. I twist-turn around so it undo-ravels. In my spin I catch a red flash inside bare branches.

"Hello, Robin!" I say. "Will it snow? Do you know?"

She hops forward ... head this side, that side, like she's thinking.

Femi's loud laugh makes Robin fly.

"Stop messing! It's freezing." Femi grabs my scarf again. "You sure you won't trade me this for anything?"

I shake my head. "Not anything."

After tea we're lying on my bed, bellies full of Pilau rice. Femi sighs. "What will you write about for the story homework?"

"Forget homework on sleepover night. But I can tell you a snow story … only for your ears."

Femi moves near, cheek close by cheek.

"Go on then…" She is whispery and waiting.

The story is about why I always keep the robin red scarf close to me... It all began when me and Grandmother flew to Snowland on a giant metal bird. We were leaving our land forever. It was my first time in an aeroplane but I was not afraid. When the plane left the ground I lifted my arms like I was growing wings. Grandmother's eyes closed tight, her hands shook as the silver bird flew into thick white clouds.

My eyes are teary. Femi squeezes my hand. I know how she misses Teta too.

On the journey Teta was worrying about winter in Snowland.

"For snow you will need thick warm clothes. For snow you will need woollen socks with toe-spaces for your hands."

I checked in her dictionary. "You mean gloves?"

Teta ignored me and carried on.

"You will need cover for your head."

"Hat."

"For snow you must wear boots and a long woollen veil."

I checked the word for what she described, not like hijab, but something to keep your neck warm… "You mean 'scarf', Teta?" I corrected.

"I will make you such a 'scarf' item. Look! I have brought wool." Teta took a ball of red wool from her bag. She knew well that red is my favourite colour.

"I will knit it for you with my own hands. I will knit us to a new land."

When she started knitting, clicking with

her needles, her face calmed, her body calmed… Mine too.

I watched Teta knit,

and the scarf grow,

row by row.

When my tears came Teta wiped them away with the red wool scarf.

"Come now, my Rabina. We must fly forward. It is the only way for us – one old bird, one young one flying to a new land."

Femi is holding my hand again.

It is strange, the feeling of letting it out, like something too tight undo-ravelling.

Inside the airport we waited for our luggage. We looked wrong, wearing sandals and too-bright clothes. At arrivals Mina was waiting to help. Teta told me, "She is distant family, now close."

The way from the airport to the city was bright flashing lights, new buildings and old. But no snow.

"First we will go to the community centre to collect some things you'll need," said Mina.

The centre was beside a Mosque. First we drank sweet hot chocolate, then Teta went to pray. Mina took me to choose a big puffer coat, boots ... and a scarf.

"Good, but no need of scarf for Rabina!" Teta said when she saw my warm clothes. She showed Mina the scarf she started knitting on our journey from the old land to the new.

"What a pretty colour," Mina said. "Robin red breast red!"

"What is robin?" I asked Mina.

She told me, "The robin is my favourite bird in this country. A friendly bird of winter. It never treats you like a stranger."

Outside Mina's flat the first thing I saw was a robin bird hop, hopping on the ground.

"Look! Look!" I cried. "Robin Red Wool

Breast come to welcome!"

Mina's smile was kind as all my words came undo-ravelling together.

That night I listened through the wall and heard Teta's needles click-click the robin red breast wool. I walked to the window, opened the curtain and...

White

      flowers

   floated

       from the sky and

  landed on the earth

     like blossom.

Am I dreaming? Then I saw wings, a red flash, a round pudding belly, heard a small, sweet welcome song.

On the edge of the window Robin Red Breast came to land.

"Did you bring my wish for snow?" I asked.

Robin placed her head this side and other side … like she tried to understand my language. Then she flew.

In the morning I woke in Snowland, holding Robin's welcome song in my heart.

"Morning, Robin, my friend!" I spoke too loud so timid robin flew away again.

For one whole day I looked for my new friend and watched the snow flowers float and fall. I wanted to fly out into the snow too, to feel it, taste it, but Teta was afraid to slide and fall.

"Sorry, Rabina, I am too old. It is too cold. And I must finish this scarf before you

go to school. You can't go without it," Teta
said.

On Monday Teta wrapped the scarf round
my neck, round and round. Still it was too
long, falling to the ground. She tied it at
my middle, over my breast.

"Now you will not get cold."

But still I shivered as I stepped outside.

So much to learn and know.

New

Footprints

My footprints

Walking a new path

Feeling nervous

Feeling alive

Ravelled in Teta's robin red scarf.

First day of school was so many people, smiles and friendly faces but I didn't understand many things. Only there were a few names I remembered...

My name is Malika

My name is Cam

My name is Loretta

"My name is Femi. Do you want some help with that ... scarf?"

On the walk home with Mina, wrapped close in Teta's scarf, I felt ice-cold, missing all the things I had to hold so tight inside.

Mama's song

Papa's laugh

Cousin Memet's toothless grin

My bed

Smell of Mama's thyme bread

Then I noticed tiny twig tracks ...

bright red tear drops.

Blood drops.

I pulled on Mina's hand and together we followed...

Robin

Red

Blood

Tracks.

By the railings we found Robin lying in the snow, one wing wounded, the other wing moving, trying hard to fly. Robin was in a panic, her heartbeat of fear made a drum of her breast. Mine too.

"Please don't cry, my welcome bird," I whispered. Robin shook, head hiding under her good wing, but she did not hop away.

"I am afraid that wing is broken," I told Mina. She stepped closer but Robin sang a song of fear.

I cried and cried and my hot tears melted snow. I bent low and the robin let me come closer.

"Robin red breast, you are afraid, I know, but my Teta made a nest..." I whispered and undo-ravelled my scarf, and ever so slowly Robin let me slide the wool under her body. I said, "Come, Robin, we must try to fly forward together."

Mina drove us to a vet's place.

Please please Robin don't die. Please let her fly.

Robin's wing was not broken … only wounded. The vet tried to give her medicine for pain, but Robin was in a panic. I sang to Robin and after a little time she grew calm.

"She seems to know your voice, Rabina," the vet lady said.

Robin placed her head this way, that way but let the vet paint painaway cream on her wing.

"It will take time to heal but we cannot keep birds here." The vet gave us a card of a place where we could take the bird for "sanctuary". But it was too far away.

"We cannot leave your grandmother alone any longer."

"Please let us look after our welcome friend till she is ready to fly! Like you look after me," I pleaded with Mina.

"And when you are at school and I'm at work?"

"Then Teta will look after her," I promised. "That way she will not feel alone."

For the first week in Snowland, Robin lived on the nest of Teta's wool. We took good care of her, fed her seeds and water. She would come close only if I sang my mama's song.

"Look!" Teta said when Robin sang back. "This bird knows our language!"

Teta and Robin sat in the window, and

followed my path to school and back in the snow. They were waiting the day I walked across the snow-melt with my first human friend in Snowland … Femi!

"Teta waving out of the window with a robin sitting on her head! How can I forget?" Femi laughed.

I giggled. "How happy she was that I wasn't alone in school."

"It's good you have a new friend, that is the best way to belong in this land. We are only beginning," Teta said. "But this Robin bird is ready to fly forward. It is wrong to keep her. We must let her go free."

"I bet she won't stray far!" Mina said, and made a bird table outside the window and a net of nuts and seeds for feeding.

That day we carried Robin Red Breast out on Teta's scarf. Her wings fluttered and Robin hopped away to peck the food on the table.

"Fly forward, friend," I called.

"It feels warmer today!" Teta said. "I too am ready to walk a little way."

The air is silent when I wake. I take slipper-steps to the window as Femi sleeps.

Robin sits on the snow-cake table to feed like every day since the summer day when Teta flew away.

We are in Snowland.

Mina bought the new robin red wool I asked for...

Today I will start to knit a scarf for Femi.

"Wake up, Femi!" I call. "No homework!"

THE MUDDLED
CHRISTMAS
MESSAGE

Katy Cannon

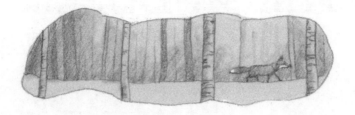

There was something different about the woods that Christmas Eve. All the animals could feel it – Finn the fox cub most of all. It made him jump and spin with anticipation.

Something was happening. Something new.

Grandad Frank gathered all the foxes together by the largest oak tree, Grandma Fern at his side.

"Christmas is a time for family." Frank's booming voice echoed off the trees, rattling the icicles hanging from the branches. Finn tried to sit still and listen – Grandad

Frank always said that Finn closed his ears when he started moving. But he couldn't stop his tail thumping in excitement. "In that spirit, this Christmas I am inviting all our family to celebrate with us. Including my brother Fergus and his family."

Whispers went up among the foxes. This was big news! Frank and Fergus hadn't spoken to each other in years and years – not since before Finn was even born. Nobody knew why the brothers had fallen out but there were lots of stories.

Now Finn would get to meet all his relatives! Maybe he had cousins who would play with him. That would be the perfect Christmas present.

"I need a responsible, reliable fox to deliver this very important invitation,"

Grandad Frank went on. "Do I have any volunteers?"

"Me!" Finn shouted enthusiastically. "I'll go!"

The foxes around him barked with laughter. "You? You're far too small. He'll never send you," one of them said.

Grandad Frank looked kindly down at Finn. "I think this job requires an older fox, little cub."

"One who can stay still long enough to listen," Grandma Fern added with a soft smile.

Finn sank down to his haunches. He so wanted to be the fox to take the message to the other side of the wood. It would be such an adventure!

"I will take the message." Felix, a stately

older fox, stepped forward.

Finn listened very carefully as Frank gave Felix his instructions.

"You must travel to the edge of our territory and deliver my message to the badger," Frank said. "Ask him to get this message to Fergus: 'Join us for Christmas, brother, and let old arguments be forgotten.' Can you remember that, Felix? It's very important."

Felix dutifully repeated the message back and Frank smiled.

"Then it's time for you to go! Give my regards to the badger."

With a small nod, Felix trotted off. When he was sure no one was watching, Finn followed.

After all, nobody had said he couldn't go with Felix. And Finn had never been to the edge of the foxes' territory before...

Felix rolled his eyes when he noticed Finn, but otherwise ignored him. Finn scampered after the older fox, enjoying the way the frost twinkled on the trees and crunched under his paws. It was a long way to the edge of the territory but just when Finn thought they'd be walking all night, Felix came to a halt.

Finn slid to a stop a moment after, landing in front of the biggest badger he'd ever seen.

"You have a message for me?" the badger asked, his kits playing noisily around his feet.

Felix nodded. "This is the message you must get to Fergus the fox, on the far side of the wood: 'Join us for Christmas, brother, and see that old arguments can be forgotten.'"

Finn frowned. That wasn't exactly the same message that Grandad Frank had given Felix, but it did mean the same thing.

The badger nodded his huge black-and-white striped head and turned to lumber away into the heart of the wood, the kits chasing after him. As he went, Finn heard the badger mumbling the message to himself over and over, so he wouldn't forget it. "Join us for Christmas, brother, and see that old arguments can't be forgotten."

Finn jumped up in alarm. That wasn't the same message at all! The badger must not have heard properly over the noise his kits were making with their chasing game!

He spun round to tell Felix, but the other fox was already heading back the way they'd came.

Oh no! Finn gnawed on the end of his tail as he tried to decide what to do. He could go back and tell Grandad Frank that the badger had got it wrong, but by then it might already be too late to get the right message to Fergus.

There was only one thing for it. He'd have to follow the badger and make sure the right message got through!

The heart of the woods were thicker and denser than where the foxes lived.

Finn tried to stay close as he trailed after the badger, the kits running at his side. They even let him join in their chasing game once he explained why he was there. Maybe Finn would be able to play the same game with his cousins, if he ever got to meet them.

The badger reached a glade, where the treetops had opened up again to let the starlight in. There a stag waited for him, shuffling impatiently from hoof to hoof. Finn abandoned the game and hurried ahead.

"The message for Fergus is: 'Join us for Christmas, brother, because old arguments can't be forgotten.'"

"Fine," the stag said, already moving away. "I'll pass it on to the owl. He can tell old Fergus. I've got more important things to be doing."

"Wait! The message is wrong!" Finn called out, but the stag had already galloped away.

Saying a quick goodbye to the kits, Finn chased through the trees after the stag. The Christmas moon shone down, glinting off the stag's antlers and pale coat, making him easy to follow. But the stag was very fast and Finn was soon out of breath.

He puffed and panted as he screeched to a stop in front of a tall sycamore tree, where the stag had paused.

"Wise one?" the stag called. "Where are you?"

There was a flutter of wings and a large white Snowy Owl landed on the lowest branch of the tree. "Who-o calls?" the owl asked.

"I do," the stag replied. "I have a message for Fergus the Fox from his brother, Frank. Will you take it to him?"

"I will. What is the message?"

"It's a simple one," the stag said. "'Don't join us for Christmas, brother, because old arguments can't be forgotten.'"

The owl sighed. "I see. Very well then."

"Wait!" Finn barked as the owl started to open her wings. "The message is all wrong!"

The owl stared down at him. "It is not for cubs to question their elders," she said. Then she stretched out her wings and rose off into the sky.

Finn settled his head on his paws and cried. Now what was he to do? He hadn't got the right message to Fergus and, even worse, he had no idea how to get back home again!

A prickle, pressed against his paw, made him look up. There beside him sat a small hedgehog.

"Why are you crying?" the hedgehog asked. "I could hear you from right across the glade."

Finn explained all about the muddled message and his adventures through the woods. "But now I've lost the owl and the message, and I don't know how to find Fergus," he sobbed.

"Oh, well that's easy," the hedgehog said.

"My home is very near Fergus's den. If you let me ride on your back, I can show you the way."

"Then let's go!" Finn lay down flat so that the hedgehog could climb up. "But keep your prickles to yourself!"

Finn and the hedgehog raced on through the night, full of excitement again. He was going to make everything right!

They arrived just as the owl finished delivering her message to an older fox with faded fur.

"Your brother says: 'Don't join us for Christmas, brother. Old arguments can't be forgotten.'"

"Why would my brother send me such a

message?" Fergus roared. "And at Christmas! I've half a mind to march straight over there and—"

"But that wasn't the message!" Finn shouted. The hedgehog slid off his back and scampered away, shaking with fright.

Fergus stared at him as Finn approached.

"And who are you, little cub?"

"I'm Finn. Frank's my grandad. Which makes you my—" he frowned.

"Great uncle," Fergus said.

"Great!" Finn beamed. "The important thing is, I was there when Granddad Frank gave the message to Felix, and when Felix gave it to the badger, and when the badger gave it to the stag, and when the stag gave it to the owl…" He took a deep breath. "And they all got it muddled up!"

"So what was the right message, then?" Fergus asked.

Finn blinked. What was the right message? He couldn't remember!

"It was something like… 'Come for Christmas, because old arguments are important.' No, that's not it."

Finn fought down his panic. He might not remember the exact words but he knew what Grandad had meant. The meaning of the message was what mattered.

"Grandad Frank wants you and your family to come and join us for Christmas dinner."

For a moment Finn was worried that his great uncle was going to say no. But then Fergus's face broke into a huge grin.

"Well, we'd better get going, then," he

said, "if we're all going to get there for Christmas morning."

This Christmas was the best one Finn could ever remember! The badger and his kits, the hedgehog, owl and stag had all travelled back with them to join in the celebrations. Finn had played with his new cousins and the kits the whole day long.

As night fell, Finn snuggled up between Grandma Fern and Grandad Frank, and listened to Fergus telling everyone the story of how Finn had brought him back home for Christmas.

"Well, it seems that maybe you can listen after all, Finn," Grandad Frank joked.

"Better than his grandad and great

uncle, anyway," Grandma Fern said. Frank
and Fergus looked sheepish.

"What does that mean?" Finn asked.

"It means I've been telling Frank to
make up with Fergus for years," Grandma
said. "And your great aunt Fiona has been
saying exactly the same thing to Fergus,
over on the other side of the wood! We
could have been friends years ago, if only
they hadn't been so stubborn."

Finn grinned, glad the two families
had made up at last – now he would get to
spend every Christmas with his cousins.

Still, he couldn't resist teasing his
grandad, just a little bit. "Really, Grandad.
Don't you know how important it is to
listen carefully?"

FORGETTING
THE YETI

Jeanne Willis

In the far-away frozen mountains of Tibet, a little yak herder gazed out of the window of his grandfather's old wooden hut, wondering why his father had not come home yet.

"The wind is howling like a pack of wolves," he said. "What if Pha Pa has blown off the mountain into the valley? What if he has got lost in the blizzard?"

Grandpa patted his shoulder. "You worry too much, Tashi. Your father is a fine herdsman and a good Sherpa. He has climbed in worse weather than this. I doubt that he is lost. He knows Mount Everest like the back of his hand."

Tashi watched the snow whirling in the sky and frowned. "But what if the howling isn't the wind, Grandpa? What if it's the Yeti? What if the elders in the village are right and a monstrous Yeti really exists and has eaten my Pha Pa?"

The old man smiled. "The elders are not always right," he said. "Sometimes they make things up to scare little boys. Come away from the window and sit by the fire with me. I will tell you a story."

"Does it have a happy ending?" asked Tashi, curling up next to him.

"Listen and you'll find out," said Grandpa as he began his tale.

"Once upon a mountain, many moons

ago, a little yak herder who wasn't very much older than you took his yaks up Mount Everest to graze. However, when he got to the pasture, the wild grass was already covered in snow. Hoping to find some tree buds for his cattle to eat, he drove them higher up the mountain along a narrow track he had never taken before.

"He had only gone a little way when suddenly the weather changed. As the temperature dropped to fifteen degrees below freezing, a wicked wind began to whistle and whipped his hat away. The little herder quickly gathered his yaks together and went to drive them home, but the wind had other ideas. As it roared and raged around the mountain ridge at a hundred miles an hour, there was a deafening crack and as the boy turned, he saw a great tide of snow hurtling towards him. The yaks scattered to safety but the boy could not run as fast as they could and he was buried under the avalanche."

Grandpa paused and lit his pipe.

"Oh dear!" wailed Tashi. "What if the same thing has happened to my Pha Pa? Is that the end of the story?"

"No," said Grandpa. "That is just the beginning! The boy was still alive under the snow. There was a pocket of air so he could breathe but he was trapped and would not have survived for much longer if someone hadn't come along and found him."

"Ah, a Sherpa rescued him," said Tashi. "They are the best climbers in the world."

"No, it wasn't a Sherpa," said Grandpa. "The boy had almost passed out from the cold. He had no hat, remember, and his ears were frozen. But just when he thought he would never see his family again, he heard a scraping sound above his head. At first he thought it was a yak digging for leaf shoots with its cloven hooves but he was mistaken. To his horror, a huge pair of hairy hands broke through the thick snow and with the strength of six men, it grabbed him and hauled him out!

"If the boy's mouth had not been stuffed with snow, he would have screamed. Crouching over him in the moonlight was a massive ape-like creature with coarse red fur, glowing eyes and the biggest feet he'd ever seen. It sniffed his clothes, brushed the icicles out of his hair and bared its yellow fangs in an almost-human grin."

"Was it the Yeti?" gasped Tashi.

"It was," said Grandpa. "And believing it wanted to eat him for supper, the boy scrabbled to his feet and tried to escape. But the frost had bitten his toes so badly, he could hardly stand and fell on to his back in the snow. The creature watched him quizzically, then with a grunt and a snort, it snatched him up, threw him over its left shoulder and ran off up the mountain."

"Did it eat the boy?" asked Tashi, his eyes wide in horror.

"Eat him?" exclaimed Grandpa. "No, no. It fed him. It carried him to its cave out of the icy wind, wrapped him in a bearskin and gave him warm yak milk to drink from a stone saucer."

"That was kind," said Tashi.

"It was kind and gentle and clever," said Grandpa. "It pulled off the boy's boots as he was shivering too hard to do it himself and rubbed his frozen feet until they were nice and pink again and blew on his ears with its hot breath to thaw them out. The boy was exhausted from his adventure and seeing that the Yeti meant him no harm, he closed his eyes and fell asleep in its arms."

"Was it really a Yeti?" asked Tashi.

Grandpa puffed on his pipe, deep in thought. "It never said it wasn't ... but how could it? Although it was like a human in many ways, it could not speak the boy's language and the boy could not speak Yeti. Even so, both knew what the other was thinking, just as the yak and the herder understand each other. This is why the Yeti decided to carry the boy back down the mountain as soon as the weather got better. As much as it loved him, it knew he belonged with his own kind and could not get home by himself."

"I expect the boy's family were very pleased to see him," said Tashi.

Grandpa sighed. "Yes but alas, his Pha Pa was not pleased to see the Yeti! The boy had been missing for days. His father was searching desperately for him but all he could find was his hat. He thought he would never see his son again but he didn't give up. He called out his name again and again, climbing higher and higher where the air is so thin only a yak herder born on the mountain can breathe.

"Up. Up. Up... Then, to his terrible shock, he saw the Yeti coming down! It had a child flung over its shoulder and recognizing his lost boy, the father raised his gun and with a trembling hand, he pointed it at the Yeti's heart and cocked the trigger.

"'Don't shoot, Pha Pa!' cried the boy. 'He is not carrying me away, he is carrying me back to you! He dug me out of the snow, he fed me and kept me safe and warm.'

"The father watched in amazement as the Yeti placed the boy back on the ground and the boy flung his arms around the creature and hugged it.

"'You see, Pha Pa? He's my friend. He just wants to live on the mountain in peace, but I am afraid for him. If you tell the elders he exists, they will not believe he is gentle and kind and they might hunt him down!'

"Realizing that the Yeti had saved his son's life, the father fell at the Yeti's feet and thanked him.

"'I will not tell the elders that I have seen you,' he said. 'We will keep the secret and keep you safe, just as you kept my son.'

"He reached into his pocket, pulled out a sweet, ripe apricot and placed it in the Yeti's giant leathery palm. With a soft grunt, the Yeti took it and sniffed it and gave an almost-human smile, as if it understood that the apricot was not just a gift – it was a golden promise."

"Did the boy ever see the Yeti again?" asked Tashi.

"No," said Grandpa. "They hugged goodbye and it stood and watched them go back down the mountain. But when the boy turned to wave, it had gone."

"Did he ever go looking for it?" said Tashi.

"He did," said Grandpa. "Every year, on the date that the Yeti saved his life, he went back up the mountain and left apricots in its cave as a sign that the promise had been kept. He never found his old friend but he knew he was there because the apricots were eaten."

"What became of the little yak herder?"

wondered Tashi. "Did he grow up and have a family of his own?"

"He did," said Grandpa. "And when he became too old to climb, he told his boy the same story that I am telling you now. And that son carried on the promise and made the same journey, year after year, to honour the Yeti. That is why your Pha Pa is on the mountain now. As you can see, the apricots have gone from the bowl."

"Oh!" gasped Tashi. "If my Pha Pa is the son of the little yak herder who is now too old to climb, you were the boy in the story!"

Grandpa stood up, rubbed his creaky knees and went over to poke the fire.

"That much is true," he said, glancing out of the window. "Ah, here comes your father now, safe and sound."

Tashi rushed to greet him.

"Pha Pa! I know where you've been!" he said. "And I know why. When you are too old to climb, I will go into the mountain every year and leave a golden promise for the Yeti too … but how will I know which cave belongs to him?"

"That's easy!" Grandpa chuckled. "It is full of apricot stones!"

THE CHRISTMAS PURR

Leila Rasheed

"Dinner's ready!"

The yell startled me awake. Was I back in the shelter? But the shelter didn't smell of roast potatoes.

"Coming, Mum!" shouted a voice.

Not the shelter. But not safe, either. Over my head, doors banged and feet thumped. I huddled down in the cardboard box, fur prickling, whiskers shivering, tail flick-flick-flicking. I sat up and peered over the edge. Christmas lights: flickering, dizzying and bright, a family hurrying to the table in a jangle of happy voices.

"Dinner, Hob." A bowl was plonked down nearby.

A big old lump of a dog, all leathery nose and slobbery tongue like a saggy brown sofa, shambled up and stuck his nose into the bowl. He gave me a wink. Then the one called Mum came in again. I hid. She put a bowl by the box and went out.

That bowl smelled like turkey. I put one paw out of the box before remembering. You can't trust anyone. I'd stay in this box until they'd all gone to bed. And then...

"Poor cat," said the kid. "She's scared. But I wish she'd come out from the utility room."

Of course I'm scared, I thought.

"Just let her be," said Mum. "She'll get to trust us."

That's what you think, I thought grimly.

"So what do you want for Christmas?" Mum said, putting on a cheerful voice.

"I just want socks," said the kid.

There was a pause.

"Christmas doesn't work that way," said Mum gently. She sounded sad.

Weird family, I thought. What kid asks for socks for Christmas? And why does Mum sound so sad about it?

Finally they were all in bed. I jumped out of the box and padded over to the bowl. I ate my turkey with one ear on the door. I was half way through it when an eye appeared at the crack of the door. It was the kid, a girl in red pyjamas, brown hair falling in tangles. I was back in the box like a rocket.

"Sorry you're scared, cat," whispered the girl. "I came down to give you Doggie. He stops me being scared."

She pushed a large raggedy object into the box.

"Stay in the box as long as you like. Mum put it there specially."

Huh. I didn't realize she put it there on purpose. It was a funny, warm feeling to know that they knew I might just want to hide deep down in something and feel safe.

No, I told myself. Trusting is dangerous. I turned my back on the girl and tried to ignore her.

The kid went out, leaving the door open. I peeked over the side of the box. She lifted down a picture from the mantelpiece. She brought it over to the box and showed it to me. It was a photograph of a black cat with white socks, wearing a red collar with a golden bell.

"This is Socks," she said. "He was my cat. I loved him lots. Then he got ill. The vet said…" She stopped and rubbed her eyes with her pyjama sleeve. "I miss him. You'd have liked him."

Oh.

I couldn't help stretching my head out and giving her hand a tiny, friendly nuzzle.

After all, she was sad.
And it was Christmas.
It didn't mean I was
going to stay.

I tried to purr, just
the start of a purr in my
throat, but it melted as quickly as a single
snowflake. I hadn't purred for nearly a
year. Not since that rainy night in January.

After the kid went back upstairs, I crept
into the sitting room. In a couple of jumps,
I was on the table, then on the window-
sill. I pushed aside the curtain. Cold hit
my nose.

It was snowing.

I stared at the big flakes drifting down.

The pavement was white and so was the road.

"Looks like it's settling."

I nearly jumped out of my fur.

It was Hob. He was lying in his basket, by a pile of shiny presents. His eyes glinted in the fairy lights.

"Oh. Sure." I sat down and licked my paw just to show him I hadn't really been scared.

"Might be a white Christmas," Hob rumbled. "I haven't seen one of those since I was a pup!"

I sniffed and moved on to the other paw.

"Yeah, that was a good Christmas. I got a rubber chicken," Hob went on, chin on his paws.

Oh my tail, I thought. *This one isn't going to shut up.* I did the rest of my paws, trying not to listen.

"... stocking of my very own ... ball ... rag toy ... half a marrow bone ... sick everywhere... Boy, those were the days!" Hob chuckled.

I hadn't got any paws left to wash and the snow was a blizzard now. I couldn't even see the other side of the road. My heart sank. I couldn't leave yet.

"So you're staying up for midnight too?" Hob said.

"What happens at midnight?"

Hob sat up straight. His eyes gleamed. His nose shone.

"Magic," he said in a voice stuffed as full of Christmas as a mince pie.

"Magic?"

Hob nodded solemnly. "When Christmas Eve turns to Christmas Day."

"What … what sort of magic?"

"I don't know. I try every year to stay up, but…" He yawned. "See?"

I shook my head. The Christmas before, it hadn't snowed. It rained. And rained and rained. Until my purr was washed away.

"I hate Christmas," I said.

I hadn't meant to say it out loud, but I could see from Hob's face that I had.

"How, ow, ow," he almost howled, "can you hate Christmas?"

I prickled all over. I didn't want anyone to feel sorry for me. If he felt sorry for me, then I might start to like him. If I liked him, I might trust him. If I trusted him, I might stay. And if I stayed... Well, that was a risk I couldn't take.

"Presents!" barked Hob. He was trying to find something I liked about Christmas.

"No one cares about presents."

"Course they do! Sam's been after that train set for months."

"He'll get bored with it by —" I swallowed

– "January 6th."

"Huh?"

"Then he'll drive it to the dump," I
went on. The brightness of the snow was
burning my eyes, or maybe it was the tree
lights. "Shove it out there and slam the car
door. And go home and it'll never see him
again."

Hob was just listening, just looking. His
big stupid trusting face. Didn't he know
you can't trust anyone?

I stalked off to the other room and stared
out at the snow. It had to stop falling soon.
Then I could go. Be on my own again, like
I was supposed to be. *Maybe I'll find my purr
out there somewhere*, I thought.

Across the road, a car door slammed.
And suddenly I was back there, in the car as

it swerved round bends, my family having an argument I didn't understand. The car braked. Why were we stopping here?

A hand grabbed the scruff of my neck and swung me out on to the wet, cold road. I fell into a puddle, mewing in confusion. I caught a last glimpse of my family before the car door slammed shut. Then the car drove off.

I sat there waiting for them to come back.

I waited.

And waited.

And waited.

"Christmas is a time for giving," Hob said behind me, startling me out of my memory.

I swung round, claws out. He stepped back.

"I was a Christmas present," I hissed at him. "How do you think I ended up at the shelter? Christmas isn't a time for giving. It's a time for throwing things away. Things like me."

I raced off to my box and hid under Doggie.

A nose snuffled me out. Hob.

"This family would never throw you away," he said gently. "We need a cat in the family. Especially Mariam."

I buried down deeper into the toy.

"You could be part of the family. Just like Socks was."

I said nothing. Mariam must be the girl who gave me Doggie.

Hob lay down on the cold floor next to my box. After a long while, I realized he wasn't going to go away.

Maybe that's when the magic started to happen.

Suddenly I was awake. Hob was snoring on the floor beside me.

I got out of the box and went into the sitting room. The clock hands were close together, pointing up. The snow had stopped falling. Outside the world was shining, silent.

I took a deep breath. Then I scurried back and nudged Hob in the side.

"Wake up," I hissed at him. "It's nearly midnight."

Hob snuffled and his eyes opened.

"I'm off," I muttered, backing away.

"Off? Where?"

But I was already on my way to the cat flap. Was I really going to do this? Was I going to leave Hob – and Mariam?

I took a deep breath and pushed the cat flap open.

The cold hit me – a tingle down my spine that gave every hair a secret, icy shiver. I lifted a paw to step on to the snowy path but when I looked to the garden gate...

A black cat with white socks stood there. He was purring. I'd never heard such a purr. It was like fire, catching light to everything with fierce, warm love like a sunrise. But that wasn't what made me stop in my tracks.

He was wearing a red collar with a golden bell.

"Socks?" I whispered.

But … the lamp-light was shining through him. As if he wasn't really there.

He met my gaze. I trembled all over at the light in his ghostly green eyes.

Look after her, he purred without speaking.

And then a car turned into the road and I was dazzled by the headlights, and when the car had gone, so had Socks.

But there were cat paw prints in the snow. And I could still hear him purring. It was so strong, that purr! It was as if it was inside me, as if, as if...

As if it was my purr.

My purr!

The purr flickered deep in my throat and chest like a candle flame. I turned, very carefully, as if I were sheltering it.

Slowly, so as not to blow the purr out, I stepped back into the house. With every second, the purr felt stronger.

Look after her.

I went upstairs two at a time. I found the kid's door and nudged it open. I hopped on to the bed next to her and curled up on the duvet near her feet, purring and purring.

I'll stay for an hour, I thought. *No longer...*

But I was still curled up there purring when I woke on Christmas morning.

ERWIN
AND LUCIA

Michael Broad

"… and then your great, great grandpa jabbed that mean old wolf in the bottom with his antlers!" said Erwin's dad. The moose swung his own large antlers and bashed a low tree branch, showering his son with snow.

"What happened then?" asked Erwin. His parents had been telling scary stories about wolves all afternoon and this one was his favourite.

"Well, they say the wolf yelped so loud that it echoed through the mountains – mountains – mountains!" said Dad, changing his voice so it sounded like a distant echo. "And the wolves never troubled him again."

"Great, Great Grandpa must have been very brave," said Erwin. "If I ever meet a wolf I'll jab him in the bottom too!" He galloped around his parents, jabbing his imaginary antlers at an imaginary wolf.

"But the point of the story is to stay away from wolves," said Mum, nudging Dad.

"Yes, that's the real lesson!" Dad said quickly. "Wolves are very dangerous. Listen to the forest and look out for their grey fur and pointy ears darting between the trees. And if you do see a wolf you must always hide or run away."

"I will," said Erwin, dashing off to find a wolf to hide or run away from.

"And don't go too far!" Mum called after him.

"I won't!" Erwin called back. "Though I wish I had an exciting wolf story of my own," he whispered to himself as he climbed up snowdrifts and stalked around pine trees. But he knew there were no wolves around. His mum and dad were so good at listening out for danger that he'd never even seen one.

Erwin was so busy searching for adventure that he didn't notice how far he'd travelled or that the snow was falling harder. The young moose had lost his way before and had always followed his own tracks back – but this time they were all covered over by the heavy snowfall.

"I don't want an adventure anymore," said Erwin as the wind began to whistle through the trees. The sun had almost set and he was feeling very small in the large twilight forest. He knew not to call out because it might attract a wolf, so Erwin crept though the trees, twitching his large ears at every sound and searching the moonlit snow. He was looking for tracks, his own or those belonging to his parents, but the ones he found were made by wolves. And there were lots of them.

Erwin saw a wide circle of paw-print tracks all around him, threading in and out of the surrounding trees and bushes. It looked like a wolf pack was searching for something, and the snow was falling so hard he knew the tracks were fresh.

A twig snapped in the distance and Erwin froze, flicking his ears in that direction. He heard panting breath and the crunch of paws on snow, then he quickly hid behind a bush, holding his breath as he peeped through the low branches.

Erwin expected a large pack of wolves to appear, snarling and drooling like those in his dad's stories. So he almost gasped when a lone wolf cub crept into the clearing. She was panting hard, like she was tired from having made all the tracks by herself, and sat under the bush to catch her breath. The wolf cub looked every bit as scared as Erwin felt and he could hear her whimpering softly. Seeing her large ears droop sadly in the moonlight, he immediately felt sorry for her. The young moose recalled his parent's warnings, but he couldn't just watch another animal in distress. Erwin gave up his hiding place and stepped into the open.

"Hello," said Erwin, keeping his distance, just in case she turned out to be mean like the wolf from the tale with his great, great grandpa. "I'm sorry to bother you, but are you all right?"

"I'm fine," said the cub as she quickly sniffed back her tears.

"My name's Erwin," said Erwin, lowering his head in a sort-of bow.

"Lucia," said the wolf cub, nodding politely.

"Pleased to meet you, Lucia," said Erwin. "Are you sure you're all right?"

"To be honest, I'm a little lost." Lucia shrugged, shaking the snow off her fur. "I was playing away from the pack and the snow came in from nowhere..."

"The same thing happened to me!" said Erwin. "Now I can't find my parents."

"I'm sorry to hear that," Lucia said kindly.

"I'm sorry you got lost too," said Erwin. "What a mess we're both in."

"Well, at least we're not alone anymore," Lucia added brightly.

"I guess so." Erwin frowned. "But I'm meant to stay away from wolves."

"I suppose that's sensible. Everyone knows that wolves and mooses can't really be friends," said Lucia, thinking hard. "But these are special circumstances, aren't they?

I already feel better having someone to talk
to. How about you?"

"I do feel a bit better," Erwin confessed.

"Good!" Lucia smiled. "Because I'm just
the friend you need."

"What do you mean?"

"I think I can help find your parents,"
said Lucia.

With this the wolf cub lifted her black
nose high in the air, turned her head this
way and that, and trotted around in a
peculiar dance. She seemed to follow
wherever her nose wanted to go, even if that
was where her new friend was standing.

"What are you doing?" asked Erwin,
hopping out of her way.

"The weather is too bad for me to find
my own parents, because I've lost their

scent and can no longer track the pack along the ground," Lucia explained. "But my nose is always good enough to sniff out mooses."

"I managed to hide from you," Erwin stated proudly.

"Actually, you didn't," said Lucia.

"Oh…" Erwin swallowed.

"This way!" Lucia said cheerfully and set off through the trees. "They do seem to be quite far off but the scent is strong. I imagine that's because they are working so hard looking for you."

"I suppose so," said Erwin, trotting alongside. He thought about his parents and how worried they must be. "Your mum and dad are probably out looking for you too, I expect."

"I can't find their scent so they must be searching beyond the forest, but I don't know which way they've gone." Lucia sniffed the icy air and changed direction. "And it's much too cold to wait out in the open."

"I'm sure my mum and dad will look after you when they find out how you helped me," said Erwin. And while he was sure that was true, he was unsure how they might react when he returned with a wolf.

The unlikely pairing of moose and wolf ran through the night forest, swapping stories to raise their spirits and so they wouldn't lose each other in the blinding blizzard. They covered a lot of ground and felt like they were the only creatures in the whole forest.

"It is getting awfully cold," said Lucia,

her teeth chattering as the freezing wind began to bite through her soft young coat. "Everyone else must have seen this weather coming."

"We do seem to be the only animals out in it," Erwin agreed.

"Not quite," said Lucia. She stopped in a small clearing and looked ahead.

Erwin drew along beside her and followed the wolf cub's gaze. Through a thick veil of swirling snowflakes the young moose could just make out two shapes forming in the dim grey moonlight. First he saw his dad's proud antlers turning as he searched among the trees, and then caught sight of his mother's worried face.

"Mum! Dad!" he yelled. "Over here!" Erwin raced towards his parents who

huddled around him to shield him from the
wind and share the warmth of their bodies.

"We searched all over," said Mum,
nuzzling his face.

"However did you find us?" asked Dad.

"My friend found you!" said Erwin,
pushing his way back out into the wind.
But as he scanned the clearing Lucia was
nowhere to be seen. "She was right behind
me!"

Erwin's parents ran after him as he
dashed about looking for his friend. Finally
he spotted Lucia curled up in the snow,
drifts forming around her small body.

"Oh goodness," said Mum. "We have to warm the poor thing."

"Let's get her out of the snow," said Dad, and lifted the wolf cub gently by the scruff of her neck. They made their way to shelter under the wide, low hanging canopy of an old pine tree.

"I never would have found you without Lucia," said Erwin, crouching next to his friend as she lay on a soft bed of pine needles. His parents gathered round to keep them warm, and everyone sighed with relief when Lucia eventually stirred and stretched. She opened her bright blue eyes and looked about.

"Did we find the right moose?" she asked Erwin hopefully.

"Yes," he smiled. "This is my mum and dad."

Erwin's parents made a big fuss of Lucia,
feeding her winter berries and making
sure she was well enough when she got up
and moved around. The wolf cub was
grateful but once the blizzard died down,
she was keen to find her own family.

"Follow us," said Erwin's parents.

The moose family and the wolf cub
headed back out into the snowy night.

"What are they doing?" asked Lucia
as Erwin's parents moved quickly uphill,
ploughing a path through the deep snow,
their ears turning and twitching, as the
young ones tagged along behind.

"Listening," whispered Erwin. "They
can hear everything."

Lucia couldn't hear anything until they
came up over the last hill and she caught

the sad cries of two familiar voices howling at the moon. Her parents had left the pack to find her and were now out on a rocky outcrop, calling out to her.

When they saw their cub, the wolves raced down to the edge of the forest where Lucia bounded out to them. They huddled and howled for joy as Lucia told them everything that had happened. The two families kept their distance and nodded respectfully, because everyone knows wolves and mooses can't really be friends. Then they turned and went their separate ways.

As the mooses headed back into the trees, Erwin had to content himself with having the best wolf story ever, though he also knew he would miss Lucia very much.

The young moose looked back just in time
to see the wolf cub bounding back towards
him while her parents waited. She skidded
to a halt in a shower of snow and they
rubbed their cheeks together.

"Friends forever?" Lucia whispered in
his ear.

"Friends forever," said Erwin.